THE OPPOSITE ZOO

Il Sung Na

ALFRED A. KNOPF
NEW YORK

The sky is DARK, and the
Opposite Zoo is CLOSED.

But the monkey's door is OPEN!
Time to explore. . . .

AWAKE!

asleep . . .

Hairy

Bald

Tall

short

shy

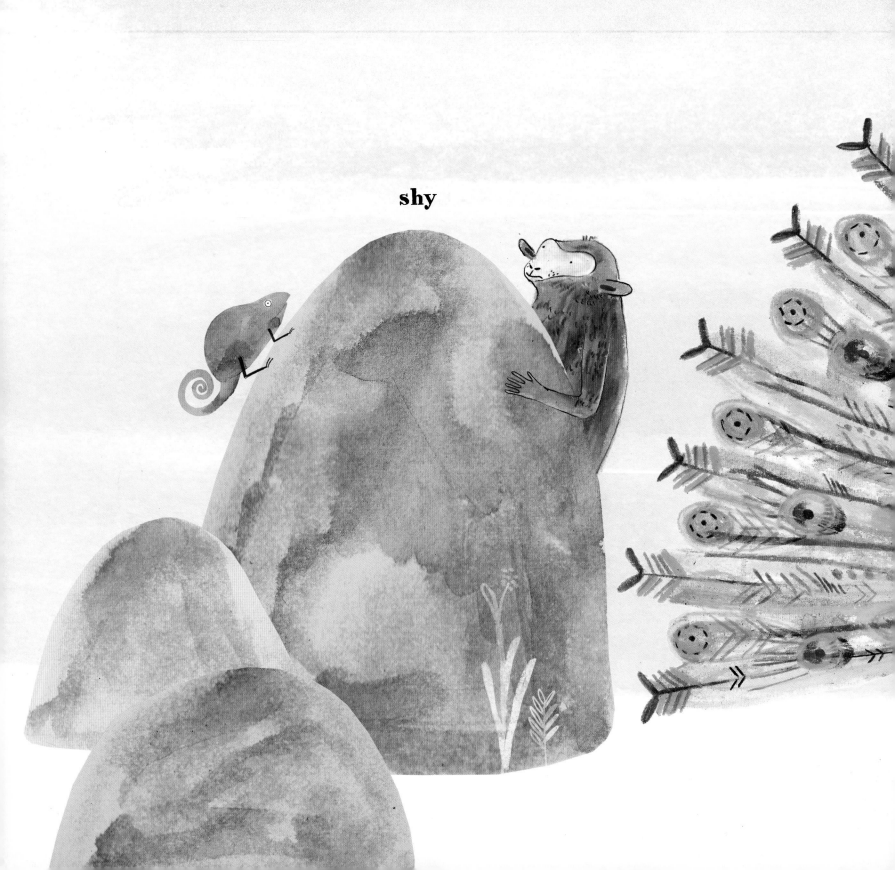

BOLD

Soft

prickly

Black

White

Slow

Fast

quiet

The sun is **BRIGHT**, and the animals are ready!

**The monkey's door CLOSES
just in time . . .**

THE OPPOSITE ZOO

. . . for the Opposite
Zoo to OPEN!

To all who inspired me to try opposites

THIS IS A BORZOI BOOK PUBLISHED BY ALFRED A. KNOPF

Copyright © 2016 by Il Sung Na

Visit us on the Web! randomhousekids.com

Educators and librarians, for a variety of teaching tools, visit us at RHTeachersLibrarians.com

Library of Congress Cataloging-in-Publication Data
Na, Il Sung, author, illustrator.
The opposite zoo / Il Sung Na. — First edition.
pages   cm.
Summary: After the zoo closes, monkey slips out of his cage to explore the
zoo, introducing the reader to the other animals and the idea of opposites.
ISBN 978-0-553-51127-7 (trade) — ISBN 978-0-553-51128-4 (lib. bdg.) —
ISBN 978-0-553-51129-1 (ebook)
1. Monkeys—Juvenile fiction. 2. Zoos—Juvenile fiction. 3. Animals—Juvenile
fiction. 4. Polarity—Juvenile fiction. [1. Monkeys—Fiction. 2. Zoos—Fiction. 3. Zoo
animals—Fiction. 4. English language—Antonyms and synonyms—Fiction.] I. Title.
PZ7.N1244Op 2016
[E]—dc23
2014043816

Also available as an ebook

MANUFACTURED IN CHINA

March 2016

10 9 8 7 6 5 4 3 2

First Edition